ZPH WRITERS

2

Coming of the Dry Season

ZPH WRITERS SERIES

I Will Wait by Bertha Msora
and Kutongwa KwaDedan Kimathi
by Ngugi wa Thiong'o and Micere
Mugo are also published by ZPH.
The River Between by Ngugi wa
Thiong'o, Things Fall Apart by
Chinua Achebe and No Longer at
Ease by Chinua Achebe are
published by Zimbabwe Educational
Books and are available through
ZPH.

CHARLES MUNGOSHI

Coming of the
Dry Season

ZIMBABWE PUBLISHING HOUSE

Zimbabwe Publishing House (Pvt) Ltd,
P.O. Box 350,
Harare, Zimbabwe

© Charles Mungoshi 1972

First published by Oxford University Press 1972
First published by ZPH 1981
Reprinted 1983, 1985, 1988, 1989, 1990, 1991

ISBN 0 949932 03 5

Printed in Zimbabwe by Jongwe Press

CONTENTS

Shadows on the Wall

FATHER IS SITTING just inside the hut near the door and I am sitting far across the hut near the opposite wall, playing with the shadows on the wall. Bright sunlight comes in through the doorway now and father, who blocks most of it, is reproduced in caricature on the floor and half-way up the wall. The wall and floor are bare, so he looks like a black scarecrow in a deserted field after the harvest.

Outside, the sun drops lower and other shadows start creeping into the hut. Father's shadow grows vaguer and climbs further up the wall like a ghost going up to heaven. His shadow moves behind sharper wriggling shadows like the presence of a tired old woman in a room full of young people, or like that creepy nameless feeling in a house of mourning.

He has tried five times to talk to me but I don't know what he wants. Now he talks about his other wife. He wants me to call her 'mother' but I can't because something in me cries each time I say it. She isn't my mother and my real mother is not dead. This other woman has run away. It is now the fourth time she has run away and tomorrow he is going to cycle fifty miles to her home to collect her. This will be the fourth time he has had to cycle after her. He is talking. I am not listening. He gives up.

Now the sun shines brilliantly before going down. The shadows of bushes and grass at the edge of the yard look as if they are on fire and father's features are cut more sharply and exaggerated. His nose becomes longer each time he nods because now he is sleeping while sitting, tired of the silence.

Father dozes, wakes up; dozes, wakes up and the sun goes down. His shadow expands and fades. Now it seems all over the wall, behind the other shadows, moving silently like a cold wind in a bare field. I look at him. There is still enough light for me to see the grey stubble sticking up untidily all over his face. His stubble, I know, is as stiff as a porcupine's, but as the light wanes now, it looks fleecy and soft like the down on a dove's nestling.

I was in the bush, long ago, and I came upon two dove nestlings. They were still clumsy and blind, with soft pink vulnerable flesh planted with short scattered grey feathers, their mouths open, waiting for their mother. I wished I had corn to give them. As it was, I consoled myself with the thought that their mother was somewhere nearby, coming home through the bush in the falling dark with food in her mouth for her children.

Next day I found the nestlings dead in their nest. Somewhere out in the bush or in the yellow ripe unharvested fields, someone had shot their mother in mid-flight home.

Not long after that, I was on my father's shoulders coming home from the fields at dusk. Mother was still with us then, and father carried me because she had asked him to. I had a sore foot and couldn't walk and mother couldn't carry me because she was carrying a basket of mealies for our supper on her head and pieces of firewood in her arms. At first father grumbled. He didn't like to carry me and he didn't like receiving orders from mother: she was there to listen to him always, he said. He carried me all the same although he didn't like to, and worse, I didn't like him to carry me. His hands were hard and pinchy and his arms felt as rough and barky as logs. I preferred mother's soft warm back. He knew, too, that I didn't want him to carry me because I made my body stiff and didn't relax when he rubbed his hard chin against my cheek. His breath was harsh and foul. He wore his battered hat that stank of dirt, sweat and soil. He was trying to talk to me but I was not listening to him. That was when I noticed that his stubble looked as vulnerable as the unprotected feathers on a dove's nestling. Tears filled my eyes then and I tried to respond to his teasing, but I gave it up because he immediately began picking on mother and made her tense and tight and this tension I could feel in me also.

After this he always wanted me to be near him and he made me ignore mother. He taught me to avoid mother. It was hard for me but he had a terrible way of making mother look despicable and mean. She noticed this and fought hard to make me cheerful, but I always saw father's threatening shadow hunched hawkishly over me. Instead of talking to either of them I became silent. I was no longer happy in either's presence. And this was when I began to notice the shadows on the wall of our hut.

One day the eternal quarrel between mother and father flared up to an unbelievable blaze. Mother went away to her people. After an unsuccessful night full of nightmares with father in the hut, he had to follow her. There had been a hailstorm in the night and everything looked sad in the dripping chill of the next day. The small mealie plants in the yard had been destroyed by the storm; all the leaves torn off except the small hard piths which now stood about in the puddles like nails in a skull. Father went away without a word and I was alone.

I lay under the blankets for a long time with the door of the hut open. One by one, our chickens began to come in out of the cold.

3

There is something in a cold chicken's voice that asks for something you don't know how to give, something more than corn.

I watched them come into the hut and I felt sorry for them. Their feathers were still wet and they looked smaller and sicklier than normal. I couldn't shoo them out. They came and crowded by the fire, their little bird voices scarcely rising above the merest whisper. My eyes left them and wandered up and down the walls.

At first I couldn't see them but when one chicken made a slight move I noticed that there were shadows on the wall.

These shadows fascinated me. There were hundreds of them. I spent the whole day trying to separate them, to isolate them, but they were as elusive and liquid as water in a jar. After a long time looking at them, I felt that they were talking to me. I held my breath and heard their words distinctly, a lullaby in harmony: sleep, sleep, you are all alone, sleep and don't wake up, ever again.

I must have fallen asleep because I remember seeing later on that the sky had turned all dark and a thin chilly drizzle was falling. The chickens, which must have gone out feeling hungry, were coming in again, wet, their forlorn voices hardly audible above the sound of the rain. I knew by the multitude of shadows on the wall that night was falling. I felt too weak to wake up and for a long time watched the shadows multiply and fade, multiply, mingle and fade, and listened to their talk. Again I must have fallen asleep because when I woke up I was well tucked in and warm. The shadows were now brilliant and clear on the wall because there was a fire on the hearth.

Mother and father had come in and they were silent. Seeing them, I felt as if I were coming from a long journey in a strange country. Mother noticed that I was awake and said,

'How do you feel?'

'He's just lazy,' father said.

'He is ill,' mother said. 'His body is all on fire.' She felt me.

'Lies. He is a man and you want to turn him into a woman.'

After this I realized how ill I was. I couldn't eat anything: there was no appetite and I wasn't hungry.

I don't know how many days I was in bed. There seemed to be nothing. No light, no sun, to show it was day or darkness to show it was night. Mother was constantly in but I couldn't recognize her as a person. There were only shadows, the voices of the shadows, the lonely cries of the dripping wet fowls shaking the cold out of their feathers by the hearth, and the vague warm shadow that must have been mother. She spoke to me often but I don't remember if I answered anything. I was afraid to answer because I was alone on a solitary plain with the dark crashing of thunder and lightning always in my ears, and there was a big frightening shadow hovering above me so that I couldn't answer her without its hearing me. That must have been father.

They might have had quarrels — I am sure they had lots of them — but I didn't hear them. Everything had been flattened to a dim depthless grey landscape and the only movement on it was of the singing shadows. I could see the shadows and hear them speak to me, so I wasn't dead. If mother talked to me at all, her voice got lost in the vast expanse of emptiness between me and the shadows. Later, when I was beginning to be aware of the change of night into day, her voice was the soft pink intrusion like cream on the hard darkness of the wall.

This turned later into a clear urgent sound like the lapping of water against boulders in the morning before sunrise. I noticed too that she was often alone with me. Father was away and must have been coming in late after I had fallen asleep.

The day I saw father, a chill set in in the hut.

There was another hailstorm and a big quarrel that night. It was the last quarrel.

When I could wake up again mother was gone and a strange woman had taken her place in the house.

This woman had a shrill strident voice like a cicada's that jarred my nerves. She did all the talking and father became silent and morose. Instead of the frightful silences and sudden bursts of anger I used to know, he now tried to talk softly to me. He preferred to talk to me rather than to his new wife.

But he was too late. He had taught me silence and in that long journey between mother's time and this other woman's, I had given myself to the shadows.

So today he sits just inside the hut with the sun playing with him: cartooning him on the bare cold floor and the bare dark walls of the hut, and me watching and listening to the images on the wall. He cannot talk to me because I don't know how to answer him, his language is too difficult for me. All I can think of, the nearest I can come to him, is when I see that his tough grey stubble looks like the soft unprotected feathers on a dove's nestling; and when I remember that the next morning the nestlings were dead in their nest because somebody had unknowingly killed their mother in the bush on her way home, I feel the tears in my eyes.

It is all — all that I feel for my father; but I cannot talk to him. I don't know how I should talk to him. He has denied me the gift of language.

2

The Crow

UP THE RIVER was a crow in a nest. For days we had watched the mates building this nest with little twigs and bits of old rags. We did a lot of shooting then, and I don't know why we did not think of shooting the birds while they were still building the nest.

We do not eat crows, and birds or animals that people do not eat are associated with the night and witchcraft in our country. The crow is very greedy. In the bush we often used to come upon some nuts it had stolen out of the fields and hidden. We could have killed it because it is a thief, but its colour — black — is always frightening and it was safer to leave it alone.

But what made us want to kill that crow in its nest by the river I still don't know.

We went into the bush before sunrise that Sunday morning. The grass drooped with the weight of the heavy dew that had fallen in the night and the trees in the west showed the ripe tint of coming day. Under the trees it was still dark and a little chilly. It was very quiet and this made us quieter too. Quieter and a little afraid of things of the night and premonitions of bad things to come. One thing we were afraid of: father and mother had gone to church and left orders that we should follow. But we had planned to go hunting instead.

As I said, we were very quiet. Then suddenly out of the dark trees by the silver-hued pool the crow rose out of its nest and alighted in a tree up the river. The rushing sound of a big winged bird left our hearts palpitating for a while. Then Chiko smiled to show that it was just a crow and he was not as afraid as I was.

Quickly I said: 'The crow.'

'I know,' he said.

'Let's shoot it,' I said, and although I was afraid of my daring, I looked at him to see how he would take the challenge.

'Let's.'

We were both afraid but it was a code between us not to show each other that we were afraid.

Before we could get to the tree where it was, the crow rose again and was away to another tree further up the river. We ran after it, skirting with quick care the thorn bushes growing on the bank of the river. Now we were approaching the tree and the crow had not risen but we could not see it.

'Sh,' Chiko said.

'I'm not talking,' I answered back.

All of a sudden the branches of the tree stirred and the crow was flying back towards its nest.

'You talked. . .' Chiko accused.

'I . . .' But we were running back again. We could not see the crow but we knew it had settled in the trees where its nest was.

Under the trees we held our breath, stepped carefully so as not to snap any twigs and carefully looked into the nest.

The crow was not there.

We looked at each other. Silently we agreed that it was somewhere in these trees and silently we asked each other whether we should go on with this mad business; and again each of us was a little afraid of the other and we pretended that we were not afraid of a crow.

We went round under the trees. I saw Chiko aiming

his catapult. I could not see the crow, so my heart stretched with Chiko's catapult, knowing, as I always know when shooting birds, that the crow would see him first and the pebble would hit an empty target. It was as I thought.

'I hit it!' Chiko exclaimed.

A lone feather floated down to us but the crow was gone. In its fear, the crow might have had this one feather hooked and plucked off by a branch.

We came out into the open and saw it settling in a tree away from the river, towards the forest. This time it saw us coming, running in the open grass between the river and the forest. We would have been relieved to give it up had it flown further into the forest but it flew again towards the river and settled in another clump of trees.

'You go that way and I'll go this way,' Chiko said.

We had it between us.

I saw it first. Its mouth was open and its bird-throat moved. I could almost hear it breathing. I saw its black eye.

I tried to load my catapult and the pebble fell out of my fingers. I saw Chiko coming from the other side — only his head. He saw me loading. He must have seen it too because I heard the branches creak and the leaves rush.

'Have you hit it?' I asked.

'A branch got in my way.'

Now the crow flew a long way, still up the river, and we followed it, running.

It hid a long time in the trees and we were a long time looking for it, with it probably seeing us but not flying away, resting. And when it was rested it disturbed us again with its sudden rush.

We were getting tired but we were all of a sudden very serious about hitting it.

Again it went to the trees where its nest was but did not settle in the nest.

We saw where it went into the trees and we found it there. I aimed at its black eye. There was a soft plunk — the sure feeling of a dead hit. The bird, dislodged, made as if to fall through the network of branches but somewhere in the air between the lowest branches and the ground it stretched its wings and flew away. Several feathers floated to us.

'I hit it,' I said.

'It's got away again,' Chiko said.

'I'm sure I hit it in the leg or somewhere.'

Once again we were running. This time the crow did not fly very far and I knew I had hit it. But it always saw us first and was away before we could get to it. It flew very low: now here, now there, but we wouldn't give up. We were quite soaked with sweat and this running had ceased to be fun. It had become something that had to be done: the killing of the crow. We would have been glad if somebody had come along and told us to stop all this madness and go home. But there were only the two of us, our obsession, our fears and the crow. It had to die.

After I don't know how long, when we had almost given up hope of ever killing it, we finally hit it in the trees where it had made its nest. Both of us saw it at the same time and both of us missed it. It did not fly away. It just made a little uncomfortable movement and settled again, its mouth open and its throat moving.

Then Chiko hit it.

It fell and was caught by a branch and it settled again, one wing stretched as a chicken's is when you pluck off the big hard flight feathers.

Now it was so near that we couldn't miss it.

But we missed five times each, and felt silly when our

ammunition ran out and we had to run and collect some more pebbles by the river.

Each time a pebble flew close to it, the bird just sort of hiccupped but did not move.

It was Chiko who finally dropped it.

But it was not dead.

Its wing was broken, its leg too, and the soft feathers on its chest were matted with blood.

Now we could hear the ghastly death-sound it made and its eyes were shiny black.

We hit it several times on the ground and each time we hit it it was in the body. It was a bloody mess. We aimed for the head but we always hit it in the body.

Now, all of a sudden, something got into us and we were fighting the crow. It was no longer fun. In fact, I don't know whether there had been a single moment in the whole business when we had thought it was fun. We were grim and sweaty. We wanted it to shut off its death-voice. We were angry and a newer fear had just come into us. It seemed as if we had started something that was beyond us. In a frenzy we picked up the pebbles that we had used and hit it again and again.

But the crow would not die.

All of a sudden, its mate cawed above us. We almost ran away. But instead the bird must have heard us because it immediately flew away into the forest.

Chiko took a stick and hit the bird's head till it was all bloody.

But the crow was still alive.

I picked up a forked stick and pinned the bird's neck to the ground. I pushed and twisted but I could feel that the neck was very strong and would not snap.

We did not know what to do. We couldn't leave it like that.

Then Chiko got mad.

When Chiko is angry with anything — say a slow ox — he hits it with everything he's got — hands, head, legs, sticks, stones — and all the time he makes a sound in his throat, and if the ox won't move he bursts into tears and you can hear him cursing through his tears and hitting the ox, getting madder and madder with each whack until he bursts out into real bawling as if *he* had been hit.

He was exactly like that with this crow that would not die.

Finally we had to throw it in the river without knowing whether it was still alive or dead.

We ran out into the open. It was already midday. Chiko was crying. He had thrown his catapult into the river together with the bird. I felt shame holding mine as if to reproach him. There was no more fun in proving myself tougher than he was, so to be equal I threw my catapult after Chiko's into the river. I suddenly smelled hot blood in my nose but I wasn't bleeding. It is the way I feel when everything goes wrong and I am afraid.

3

The Mountain*

WE STARTED FOR the bus station at first cockcrow that morning. It was the time of the death of the moon and very dark along the mountain path that would take us through the old village, across the mountain to the bus station beyond. A distance of five miles, uphill most of the way.

The mountain lay directly in our path and was shaped like a question mark. I liked to think of our path as a question, marked by the mountain. It was a dangerous way, Chemai had said, but I said that it was the shortest and quickest if we were to catch the 5 a.m. bus. I could see that he did not like it but he said nothing more, to avoid an early quarrel.

We were the same age although I bossed him because I was in Form Two while he had gone only as far as Standard Two. He had had to stop because his father, who didn't believe in school anyway, said he could not get the money to send Chemai to a boarding school. We had grown up together and had become great friends but now I tolerated him only for old time's sake and because there was no one within miles who could be friends with me. Someone who had gone to school, I mean. So I let Chemai think we were still great friends although I found him tedious and I preferred to be alone most of the time, reading or dreaming. It is sad when you have grown up together but I could not help it. He knew so little and was afraid of so many things and talked

* 'The Mountain' was first published in Zuka 5, October 1970.

and believed so much rot and superstition that I could not be his friend without catching his fever.

From home the path ran along the edge of a gully. It was a deep, steep gully but we knew our way. The gully was black now and in the darkness the path along its rim was whitish. You never know how much you notice things on a path: rocks, sticking-out roots of trees, holes, etc., until you walk that path at night. Then your feet grow eyes and you skirt and jump obstacles as easily as if it were broad daylight.

On our right, away into the distance, was bush and short grass and boulders and other smaller gullies and low hills that we could not see clearly. Ahead of us dawn was coming up beyond the mountain but it would be long, not till almost sunrise, before the people in the old village saw the light. The mountain cast a deep shadow over the village.

We walked along in silence but I knew Chemai was afraid all the time and very angry with me. He kept looking warily over his shoulder and stopping now and then to listen and say, 'What's that?' although there was nothing. The night was perfectly still except for the cocks crowing behind us or way ahead of us in the old village. We barely made any noise in our rubber-soled canvas shoes. It can be irritating when someone you are walking with goes on talking when you don't want to — especially at night. There was nothing to be afraid of but he behaved as if there was. And then he began to talk about the Spirit of the Mountain.

He was talking of the legendary gold mine (although I didn't believe in it, really) that the Europeans had failed to drill on top of the mountain. The mountain had been the home of the ruling ancestors of this land and the gold was supposed to be theirs. No stranger could touch it, the people said. We had heard these things when we were children but Chemai told them as if I were a stranger, as if I knew nothing at all. And to annoy him, because he was annoying me, I said, 'Oh, fibs. That's all lies'.

He started as if I had said something I would be sorry for. 'But there are the holes and shallow pits that they dug to prove it.'

'Who dug?'

'The Europeans. They wanted to have the gold but the Spirit would not let them have it.'

'They found no gold. That's why they left,' I said.

'If you climb the mountain you will see the holes, the iron ropes and iron girders that they abandoned when the Spirit of the Mountain broke them and filled the holes with rocks as soon as they were dug.'

'Who told you all this?' I asked. I knew no one ever went on top of that mountain — especially on that part of it where these things were supposed to be.

'All the people say so.'

'They lie.'

'Oh, what's wrong with you? You know it's true but just because you have been to school you think you know better.'

I knew he was angry now. I said, 'And don't I, though? All these things are just in your head. You like being afraid and you create all sorts of horrors to make your life exciting.'

'Nobody has to listen to you. These things happen whether you say so or not.'

'Nothing happens but fear in your head.'

'Do you argue with me?' His voice had gathered fury.

'Remember I grew up here too,' I said.

'But you haven't seen the things I have seen on that mountain.'

'What have you seen?'

'Don't talk so loud.' He lowered his voice and went on, 'Sometimes you hear drums beating up there and cows lowing and the cattle-driving whistles of the herd-boys. Sometimes early in the hot morning sun you see rice spread out to dry on the rocks. And you hear women laughing at a washing place on a river but you cannot see them.'

'I don't believe it,' I said. The darkness seemed to thicken and I could not see the path clearly. 'I don't believe it,' I said again and then I thought how funny it would be if the mountain suddenly broke into wild drum-beats now. It was crazy, of course, but for no apparent reason at all I remembered the childhood fear of pointing at a grave lest your hand got cut off.

It was silly, but walking at night is unnerving. I didn't mind it when I was a kid because I always had father with me then. But when you are alone a bush may appear to move and you must stop to make sure it is only a bush. You are not quite sure of where you are at night. You see too many things and all of them dark so you don't know what these things are, for they have no voice. They will neither move nor talk and so you are afraid. It is then you want someone older, like father, to take care of things for you. There are many things that must be left unsaid at night but Chemai kept on talking of them. Of course the teachers said this was all nonsense. I wished it were so easy to say so here as at school or in your heart as in your mouth. But it would not help us to show Chemai that I was frightened too. However, I had to shut him up.

'Can't you ever stop your yapping?'

We had crossed a sort of low hill and were dropping slight-ly but immediately we were climbing sharply towards the

mountain. It loomed dark ahead of us like a sleeping animal.
We could only see its jagged outline against the softening
eastern sky. Chemai was walking so lightly that I constantly looked back to see if he was there. We walked in
silence for some time but as I kept looking back to see
whether he was there I asked him about the road that
I had heard was going to be constructed across the
mountain.

'They tried but they could not make it,' he said.

'Why couldn't they?'

'Their instruments wouldn't work on the mountain.'

'But I heard that the mountain was too steep and there
were too many sharp, short turns.'

'No. Their instruments filled up with water.'

'But they are going to build it,' I said. 'They are going
to make that road and then the drums are going to stop
beating.' He kept quiet and I went on talking. It was
maddening. Now that I wanted to talk he kept quiet. I
said, 'As soon as they set straight what's bothering them
they are going to make that road.' I waited for him to
answer but he didn't. I looked over my shoulder. Satis-
fied, I continued. 'And think how nice and simple it's
going to be when the road is made. A bus will be able
to get to us in the village. Nobody will have to carry
things on their heads to the station any more. There will
be a goods store and a butchery and everybody will get
tea and sugar and your drums won't bother anyone. They
shall be silenced for ever.'

Just as listening to someone talking can be trying, so
talking to someone who, for all you know, may not be
listening, can be tiring. I shut up angrily.

We left the bush and short grass and were now passing
under some tall dark trees that touched above our heads.
We were on a stretch of level ground. We couldn't see the

17

path here because there were so many dead leaves all over the ground and no broken grass to mark the way.

I couldn't say why but my tongue grew heavy in my mouth and there was a lightness in my head and a tingling in my belly. I could hear Chemai breathing lightly, with that lightness that is a great effort to suppress a scream; almost a catching of the breath as when you have just entered a room and you don't want anyone in the room to know that you are about.

Suddenly through the dark trees a warm wind hit us in the face as if someone had breathed on us. My belly tightened but I did not stop. I heard Chemai hold his breath and gasp, 'We have just passed a witch.' I wanted to scream at him to stop it but I had not the voice. Then we came out of the trees and were in the bush and short grass, climbing again. I released breath slowly. It was much lighter here, and cooler.

Much later, I said, 'That was a bad place.'

Chemai said, 'That's where my father met witches eating human bones, riding on their husbands.'

'Oh, you and your . . .' He had suddenly grabbed me by the arm. He said nothing. Instinctively, I looked behind us.

There was a black goat following us.

I don't know why I laughed. Then after I had laughed I felt sick. I expected the sky to come shattering itself round my ears but nothing happened, except Chemai's fear-agitated hand on my shoulder.

'Why shouldn't I laugh?' I asked. 'I'm not afraid of a goat.'

Chemai held me tighter. He was shaking me as if he had paralysis agitans. I grew sicker. But I did not fall down. We pushed on, climbing now, not steeply, but enough to make us sweat, towards the old village, into the shadow of the mountain whose outline had now become sharper. It was lighter than when we had started, probably third cockcrow, but it was still dark enough to make us sweat with fear.

'You have insulted her,' Chemai said accusingly.

I said nothing. It was no use pretending I didn't know what I was doing. I knew these goats. Lost spirits. Because I had laughed at it it would follow me wherever I went. It would eat with me, bathe with me, sleep with me. It would behave in every way as if I were its friend or, better still, its husband. It was a goat in body but a human being in spirit. We had seen these goats, as children, grazing peacefully on the hills and there was nothing in them to tell they were wandering spirits. It wasn't until someone laughed at them or said something nasty to them that they would file in a most ungoatlike manner after whoever had insulted them. And then when this happened it needed the elders and much medicine-brewing to appease them, to make them go away.

We walked on very quietly now. We came into the open near the old village school. The path would pass below the old church, and a mile or less on we would enter the village.

There would be no question of our proceeding beyond the village this morning, while it was still dark. I didn't care whether we caught the five o'clock bus or not. I just did not have the strength to cross the mountain before the sun came up.

Also I had to see my grandmother about our companion.

'Let's wait for daylight in the village,' I told Chemai. I saw his head bob vigorously in the dark.

My grandmother lived in the old village. She had refused to accompany us and many other people of the village when we moved further west to be near water. She had said this was home — our home — and she would die here and be buried here and anyone who died in the family would be brought back to the old village to be buried. She had had a long argument with my father but she had been firm.

I did not like the old village nor grandmother Jape because both of them reminded me of my childhood and the many nightmares in which I dreamed of nothing but the mountain having moved and buried us under it. And then I would scream out and wake up and the first thing I would smell was grandmother Jape's smoke-dyed, lice-infested blankets that were coarse and warmly itchy and very uncomfortable to sleep in.

I rarely paid her any visits now, and I wouldn't have stopped to say hello were it not for the goat and my fear to cross the mountain in the dark. She would know what to do.

We were now below the church.

Suddenly the church gave me an idea. It had two doors each in opposite walls. We would try to leave the goat in the church. It was a further insult but I felt the risk was worth taking.

When I told Chemai he said he did not like it.

'I shall try it anyway,' I said.

'She will not stay. She will get out.'

We went up the path leading to the church door. We went in. The goat followed. I shouted, 'To the other door, quick!'

Chemai rushed for the opposite door. The goat followed him but stopped suddenly when the door banged to in its face. I slipped through this other door and shut that one behind me too.

Free. We ran for the village a mile up the hill.

Grandmother's hut was near the centre of the village. I knew my way about and in a short time we were knocking on her door, each time looking back over our shoulders to see whether the goat had escaped. I had to say, 'It's me, Nharo' before grandmother would open for us. 'Many things walk the night with evil in their hearts,' she had once told me.

'What brings you here in the middle of the night?'

'Nothing. We are going to the bus. We want to go to Umtali.'

'To the bus at this hour? Are you mad? You must be. . .' She was looking behind us and I knew our friend had escaped. Quickly we slipped through the door, but the goat followed us into the hut.

Without saying anything grandmother was already busy with her medicine pots. And suddenly, safe and warm, I felt that the goat was harmless. It was just a wronged friend and would go away when paid. I looked at it. It was a small she-goat, spotless black. In the dim fireglow of grandmother's hut it looked almost sad.

Grandmother was eating medicines and Chemai was watching her intently. I felt safe. Somebody who knew was taking care of things at last. It is a comforting feeling to have someone who knows take care of those things you don't know.

4

The Hero

JULIUS CAME OUT of the Staff Room. Behind him, as he
went out, he was aware of the silent eyes of the Principal
and the Headmaster. He walked with a defiant limp.

Everybody had gone to their classrooms for the last
lesson of the day after the three-thirty break. The
quadrangle was deserted. Bits of white broken paper lay
scattered everywhere on the sand. Julius had the feeling
of walking through a battlefield, looking at the dead
bodies of the conquered. He felt contempt for all the conquered, whoever they were.

He walked straight to his classroom at the other end
of Block A. He knew that more than three hundred pairs
of eyes were looking at him from several windows. He
could hear cheering hisses. But he did not care for them.
He despised them all. He felt very tall. He suppressed an
impulse to whistle.

Silence was shattered when he entered his classroom.
The class teacher — who was also the Headmaster —
was still in the Staff Room. The boys eagerly stood up
and gathered round him. They fired barrels of questions
at him. But he must not appear eager to answer them. . .
A cynical lopsided grin hovered on his lips. He was disappointed that the girls did not rush to him as the boys
had done but he was pleased to see that all their starry
eyes, especially Dora's — his lovely deskmate's — were on
him. He knew they must know all the details by now and
be anxious to hear the end of it. But he would not give
it to them yet. He must be cruel to himself. He must not

care about what happened to himself. They must see him as he truly was. They must completely forget all the impressions they had gathered about him on the football field or on the race track. He felt a savage desire to avenge himself on them, to see them wince with pain as they took the blow that was the real Julius. . .

'Oh, there's nothing to tell,' he said with a non-committal sneer. Then quickly he told himself that he must not look serious because, when they discovered the truth, they might think he was crying for himself. What he did not want from anybody was pity. He was a hero and heroes are to be admired not pitied.

'They just told me to go home and never come back.'

There was a stunned silence in the classroom. Julius noticed a crumbled look come on to Dora's face and quickly said, 'Oh, it's only a joke.' And there were sighs of relief and everybody was laughing with him, saying what a time he had given the Old Bat and what a stand he, Julius, had made. Julius felt very important. He felt a secret elation for they did not yet know the truth. Once they knew that he was really going home he was certain their admiration for him would be so strong that most of them would cry. He laughed carelessly. He had never felt this way before. He made a very poor joke and everybody laughed. In his heart Julius had always felt that he would do something that would make everybody envy him. And this was his day. He remembered his anguish on the football field and on the race track. . . Oh, he had known he would square up with them somewhere, some time.

He said nothing more. He pretended not to hear his classmates talking about him as he took his books out of his desk and, after a dashing grin meant for an 'Excuse me', piled them on Dora's. He was whistling a very low tune which he knew only Dora could hear. She had once told him that she loved to hear him sing it. But he must not appear as if he was doing it for her. He must be indifferent, cruel. He knew she loved him but he must not be won so easily. He must torture her with love. . .

She could not help but see who he was now. He was not one of them. He led his own mysterious life. Mystery and danger, the key words. He was unique. He saw all the girls despising their boyfriends, throwing them away, for him. . .

He could still feel the waves of ecstasy his speech to the Principal and the Headmaster had set in motion in him.

'. . . I am not going to eat what you yourself would not willingly throw to your dog. I pay for the food here and I must have my money's worth. For a long time we have complained about the poor diet at this school, but you have plugged your ears with sealing wax. We have told your yellow prefects over and over. . .' It had been a bold speech, a dangerous speech, and no one could have made it except himself, Julius.

Dangerous. . . He was going home because he was a dangerous element in the school, the Principal had said. And, thinking of the Principal, Julius felt a warmth for the Old Man. He knew that inwardly the Principal admired his courage. He had seen the Old Man shake his head with a smile, after that speech, and look at him with such an eye as if to say, 'You will go far, my boy', and Julius had known that it was only to please the Old Bat that the Old Man was sending him home. After all, it was the Old Man himself who had nicknamed Julius Little Caesar. Julius felt sorry for the Principal because he was about to lose such a fine young man. . .

Suddenly the Headmaster came in. He looked at his

watch and said, 'All right, Julius. The ten minutes is up. Time for you to leave this holy place.' The Old Bat was in a joking mood but nobody joined him. All of a sudden everybody hated him. Julius was aware of the silent anger of his classmates against the Old Bat. He could hear rumblings and grumblings at the back of the classroom. And once again he felt very tall and so lightheaded that he nearly cried for love of all his classmates, and he was not angry with the Old Bat, but only sorry for him. But he was a hero. He must put on a show of resistance or something of that sort. . .

'Okay, okay, Bwana!' and giving a hollow, bitter laugh that sounded false rather than defiant he began to whistle . . . and from the corner of his eye he could see that Dora's eyes were very dark and tears glittered in them. . .

His heart pounding heavily with love, Julius was led out of the classroom. The Headmaster told the head boy of the school to take Julius to the dormitories and supervise his packing. And, hands thrust deep in his pockets, Julius walked tall between the two blocks of classrooms, three hundred pairs of eyes on him. He was going to pack and go. . . He was a dangerous element in the school . . . He had made a shocking speech. . . Julius could see Dora shedding a tear or two.

Later, he was standing on a little rise of the very long road to his home. He held his untidy little bundle of clothes in his right hand and with the left he shaded his eyes from the sun as he looked along that road. He felt as bad as when he had missed a ball on the football field. What he had done, he felt, had been very childish. It was not as big as he had thought. He had achieved nothing. He saw Dora's look as he had left the classroom — he had lost her too. Now somebody else was going to take her. She would not care about him now. He felt something catch in his throat. Everything lost colour. His speech had not been so wonderful after all, and he wasn't so dangerous either; the look in Dora's eyes had not been of love nor admiration but of pity. Only the last words the Old Bat had spoken to him seemed true. He was 'a poor, spoilt, blind child who needed a loving mother's care'. Julius felt very sorry for himself. Already he could hear his stepmother's bick-bickering voice. . . He felt very tired, and from this little rise of the road, he could see the whole country lying flat and desolate and its lonely black immensity chilled him. He felt very small, very insignificant, and nobody cared what happened to him. The only important things to him now were that he was going home and the sun was setting and he was alone and it was sixty miles home. . .

Thinking of the untravelled journey in front of him, he made a loud statement in the Past Third Person Singular: 'The only time he has ever been happy was when he was at school'. And after saying this, he could not help the tears that came into his eyes.

5

The Setting Sun and the Rolling World

OLD MUSONI RAISED his dusty eyes from his hoe and the unchanging stony earth he had been tilling and peered into the sky. The white speck whose sound had disturbed his work and thoughts was far out at the edge of the yellow sky, near the horizon. Then it disappeared quickly over the southern rim of the sky and he shook his head. He looked to the west. Soon the sun would go down. He looked over the sunblasted land and saw the shadows creeping east, bleaier and taller with every moment that the sun shed each of its rays. Unconsciously wishing for rain and relief, he bent down again to his work and did not see his son, Nhamo, approaching.

Nhamo crouched in the dust near his father and greeted him. The old man half raised his back, leaning against his hoe, and said what had been bothering him all day long.

'You haven't changed your mind?'

'No, father.'

There was a moment of silence. Old Musoni scraped earth off his hoe.

'Have you thought about this, son?'

'For weeks, father.'

'And you think that's the only way?'

'There is no other way.'

The old man felt himself getting angry again. But this would be the last day he would talk to his son. If his son was going away, he must not be angry. It would be equal to a curse. He himself had taken chances before, in his own time, but he felt too much of a father. He had worked and slaved for his family and the land had not betrayed him. He saw nothing now but disaster and death for his son out there in the world. Lions had long since vanished but he knew of worse animals of prey, animals that wore redder claws than the lion's, beasts that would not leave an unprotected homeless boy alone. He thought of the white metal bird and he felt remorse.

'Think again. You will end dead. Think again, of us, of your family. We have a home, poor though it is, but can you think of a day you have gone without?'

'I have thought everything over, father. I am convinced this is the only way out.'

'There is no only way out in the world. Except the way of the land, the way of the family.'

'The land is overworked and gives nothing now, father. And the family is almost broken up.'

The old man got angry. Yes, the land is useless. True, the family tree is uprooted and it dries in the sun. True, many things are happening that haven't happened before, that we did not think would happen, ever. But nothing is more certain to hold you together than the land and a home, a family. And where do you think you are going, a mere beardless kid with the milk not yet dry on your baby nose? What do you think you will do in the great treacherous world where men twice your age have gone and returned with their backs broken — if they returned at all? What do you know of life? What do you know of the false honey bird that leads you the whole day through the forest to a snake's nest? But all he said was: 'Look. What have you asked me and I have denied you? What, that I have, have I not given you for the asking?'

'All. You have given me all, father.' And here, too, the son felt hampered, patronized and his pent-up fury rolled through him. It showed on his face but stayed under control. You have given me damn all and nothing. You have sent me to school and told me the importance of education, and now you ask me to throw it on the rubbish heap and scrape for a living on this tired cold shell of the moon. You ask me to forget it and muck around in this slow dance of death with you. I have this one chance of making my own life, once in all eternity, and now you are jealous. You are afraid of your own death. It is, after all, your own death. I shall be around a while yet. I will make my way home if a home is what I need. I am armed more than you think and wiser than you can dream of. But all he said, too, was:

'Really, father, have no fear for me. I will be all right. Give me this chance. Release me from all obligations and pray for me.'

There was a spark in the old man's eyes at these words of his son. But just as dust quickly settles over a glittering pebble revealed by the hoe, so a murkiness hid the gleam in the old man's eye. Words are handles made to the smith's fancy and are liable to break under stress. They are too much fat on the hard unbreaking sinews of life.

'Do you know what you are doing, son?'

'Yes.'

'Do you know what you will be a day after you leave home?'

'Yes, father.'

'A homeless, nameless vagabond living on dust and rat's droppings, living on thank-yous, sleeping up a tree or down a ditch, in the rain, in the sun, in the cold, with nobody to see you, nobody to talk to, nobody at all to tell your dreams to. Do you know what it is to see your hopes come crashing down like an old house out of season and your dreams turning to ash and dung without a tang of salt in your skull? Do you know what it is to live without a single hope of ever seeing good in your own lifetime?' And to himself: Do you know, young bright ambitious son of my loins, the ruins of time and the pains of old age? Do you know how to live beyond a dream, a hope, a faith? Have you seen black despair, my son?

'I know it, father. I know enough to start on. The rest I shall learn as I go on. Maybe I shall learn to come back.'

The old man looked at him and felt: Come back where? Nobody comes back to ruins. You will go on, son. Something you don't know will drive you on along deserted plains, past ruins and more ruins, on and on until there is only one ruin left: yourself. You will break down, without tears, son. You are human, too. Learn to the *haya* — the rain bird, and heed its warning of coming storm: plough no more, it says. And what happens if the storm catches you far, far out on the treeless plain? What, then, my son?

But he was tired. They had taken over two months discussing all this. Going over the same ground like animals at a drinking place until, like animals, they had driven the water far deep into the stony earth, until they had sapped all the blood out of life and turned it into a grim skeleton, and now they were creating a stampede on the dust, grovelling for water. Mere thoughts. Mere words. And what are words? Trying to grow a fruit tree in the wilderness.

'Go, son, with my blessings. I give you nothing. And when you remember what I am saying you will come back. The land is still yours. As long as I am alive you will find a home waiting for you.'

'Thank you, father.'

'Before you go, see Chiremba. You are going out into

the world. You need something to strengthen yourself. Tell him I shall pay him. Have a good journey, son.'

'Thank you, father.'

Nhamo smiled and felt a great love for his father. But there were things that belonged to his old world that were just lots of humbug on the mind, empty load, useless scrap. He would go to Chiremba but he would burn the charms as soon as he was away from home and its sickening environment. A man stands on his feet and guts. Charms were for you — so was God, though much later. But for us now the world is godless, no charms will work. All that is just the opium you take in the dark in the hope of a light. You don't need that now. You strike a match for a light. Nhamo laughed.

He could be so easily light-hearted. Now his brain worked with a fury only known to visionaries. The psychological ties were now broken, only the biological tied him to his father. He was free. He too remembered the aeroplane which his father had seen just before their talk. Space had no bounds and no ties. Floating laws ruled the darkness and he would float with the fiery balls. He was the sun, burning itself out every second and shedding tons of energy which it held in its power, giving it the thrust to drag its brood wherever it wanted to. This was the law that held him. The mystery that his father and ancestors had failed to grasp and which had caused their being wiped off the face of the earth. This thinking reached such a pitch that he began to sing, imitating as intimately as he could Satchmo's voice: 'What a wonderful world'. It was Satchmo's voice that he turned to when he felt buoyant.

Old Musoni did not look at his son as he left him. Already, his mind was trying to focus at some point in the dark unforeseeable future. Many things could happen and while he still breathed he would see that nothing terribly painful happened to his family, especially to his stubborn last born, Nhamo. Tomorrow, before sunrise, he would go to see Chiremba and ask him to throw bones over the future of his son. And if there were a couple of ancestors who needed appeasement, he would do it while he was still around.

He noticed that the sun was going down and he scraped the earth off his hoe.

The sun was sinking slowly, bloody red, blunting and blurring all the objects that had looked sharp in the light of day. Soon a chilly wind would blow over the land and the cold cloudless sky would send down beads of frost like white ants over the unprotected land.

6

The Lift

WHEN THEY WERE tired of going round the factories and shops in search of jobs, the boys went to the tall buildings at the heart of the city for their daily free ride in the lifts. It was the only fun they had and it made them forget a little their burning bellies and tired feet.

There were lots of clouds flung about the sky like cotton balls in a field. It was rather chilly and the boys felt sharply the pleasant warmth of the sun when it came out of the clouds, and both of them unconsciously looked up irritably when it darted behind another cloud.

At present, their minds, usually the colour of the changing streets and just as desolate, were fixed on the ride in the lifts.

Pearl Assurance Building, one of the tallest buildings in the city, had a guard at the wide entrance.

'Can I help you?' the guard asked.

'We would like to go up.'

'Floor?'

'Tenth.'

'What for?'

The boys looked at each other and hazarded an answer.

'We are doing correspondence courses.'

The guard looked at them suspiciously and then dismissed them with a flick of the hand.

'You are not allowed up there.'

The boys looked at the guard as if they had not heard him. Then their eyes turned to gaze at the wall above the lift where numbers went on and off in amber to show the lift coming down.

'There has been much stealing up there lately,' the guard said.

'We are not thieves.'

The guard's eyes swept over their heads and he dismissed them from his attention.

'Go away, boys.'

The boys turned to go. They passed two European boys of their own age. Looking back, the boys saw the guard take off his cap to the Europeans who did not answer him and quickly entered the lift and disappeared.

'Why did you allow those two to go up?'

'*You* are not allowed up there.'

The boys went out on to the street. It was not yet noon and they had nowhere to go and nothing to do to kill the time until night when they would go home to sleep.

'Wish I had kept that shilling after all,' one of them, thinner than the other, said.

'We had to have something to eat.'

'All the same, we could have used it now. It's so much nicer to have something to eat when you don't have anything to do.'

They were moving towards Salisbury Park. They had not talked of the park yet both of them knew that that was the only place left to go and rest.

'I was a fool to use that shilling,' the thin one said again.

His friend didn't answer because he always felt irritated by his companion's mourning for things that could have been. He felt like shouting at him to stop it but he controlled himself. He didn't care for words when he was tired. They made him even more tired than he really was.

'This is unbearable,' the thin one said once more.

But his friend kept quiet. He was hungry and there was

nowhere to get money from. The thin one looked at him, knew that he would be asked why he was looking at him, and kept quiet, knowing that this would only lead to a quarrel. But all the same, it could have been so much better if his friend would talk, then he wouldn't have to think and feel that he was not wanted, so lonely and so hopeless. The park was almost deserted except for two or three people lying on the forbidden grass, asleep or pretending to be asleep.

The thin one said, 'They are going to start trouble with the authorities.'

His friend answered him this time. 'It's silly to forbid people from lying on the grass. What is it there for?'

'It's the rules.'

'To hell with the rules.'

They found a bench under some bamboos and sat down. Immediately they had sat down, the talkative one said, 'They are not allowed to lie on the grass.'

'You have said that already.'

The thin boy looked at his friend and said nothing more. His friend leaned back on the bench and closed his eyes, pretending to go to sleep but the other one knew that this was the cue for him to keep quiet. Both of them were under a strain. They wanted to be somewhere else; the swimming pool, the beer hall — anywhere where there were people and fun and a chance to forget themselves. But there was only the wide empty park and themselves. The sleepless one looked around the park. He tried to steady his thoughts on the flowers and the trees and the light in the leaves of the trees and the shadows of the trees on the grass and the tall buildings of the city beyond the trees and the immense space of sky above the city, but there was nowhere his thoughts could rest and he was forced to come back to himself. But he was tired of looking into himself, of asking himself why he was like this and not like that, tired of examining himself, of finding faults with himself, tired of judging and condemning himself. He was tired of the whole circling process of his thoughts, so tired that he wanted movement — any movement, to feel that he was going somewhere and not just stationary. The feeling of doing nothing, of being nothing, oppressed and frightened him. He must talk — at least: that gave him a sense of direction, a feeling of really moving towards something. But his friend would not talk.

'That guard was just a nuisance. We wanted nothing except a ride. Only one ride in the lift.'

His friend stirred impatiently and said, 'Perhaps he was right. Lift rides are so short anyway.'

'But sometimes you get off a lift and find the sun has set.'

'Why don't you try to get some sleep? The sun would set faster.'

'I can't sleep during the day.'

'Then shut up please and let me sleep.'

The thin boy watched his friend as he moved towards the further end of the bench after these words. He moved towards the other end and closed his eyes. But he opened them again, worried about the space between them and the empty space that had opened up in him on closing his eyes.

'Can't we do something?' he asked.

Without a word, his friend rose and walked away to another bench and sat down, staring through the trees across the park towards the city. The thin one stayed in his place and struggled to keep himself seated, afraid to stand up and follow his friend, afraid to make even the smallest movement with his body that he knew before he had made it would fall into the pattern of yesterday, today and of tomorrow. So he tried to hurry the night when the darkness would hold his thoughts together and he wouldn't be worried by the distance between their two benches, the space that isolated them; so that looking at the two of them from afar, he saw that they were not friends. Not quite friends.

7

The Ten Shillings

TWO YEARS OF tramping had hardened Paul Masaga into a cynical sceptic about his ever finding a job. He viewed his case as if it were somebody else's, without interest, with a shrug of the shoulders. He never thought seriously that he would ever work. So he had gone to the interview without any hope of success. He went so that he would not waste his time later on telling himself: 'If I had gone it might have been different.'

He had had no illusions of better times to come. His heart had not beaten as it would have done two years ago when he was still new to the city. He had grown up since then. He knew about the Europeans. They were all alike in their dealings with the African. An African would do or was bloody lazy. That was that. If they knew anything about the emotional life of an African it was that he was unstable, a potential rapist and murderer. So he had gone only to save himself regrets later on.

He was tired. He did not care what kind of work he did now. Two years of walking up and down the city. Two years of being kicked here and there in the locations. Two years of begging for food. Two years of sleeping in the gutters and drainpipes. *Mararapaipi*, they called him in the locations, pipe-sleeper.

Any day was just like another. He had forgotten how to laugh. He avoided crowded places, afraid he might run into people from home or ex-schoolmates. He avoided places where they cooked food because he would only excite a hunger he would not be able to satisfy. He had lost his Junior Certificate. He had not meant to lose it but what difference did it make? It had been just a piece of paper like any other. It had failed to get him a job while he had it. In fact, it had fooled him about his true worth. In the beginning he had gone looking for a clerical job or any of these white-collar jobs because he had trusted the certificate. People had told him that a JC would have no trouble getting a job. He had believed them. He had been hopeful and overconfident that he held the open sesame to life. He had written letters home and to school telling relatives and friends that he was now in the city — as if that were an accomplishment in itself. City-awe. That had been his disease. It was the disease of any rural African. Until they had spent a week of city-walking, city-hunger and city-cruelty. It had been humiliating to discover that he was not the only JC in the city. He had seen many of them at the Labour Exchange in Cameron Street and most of them held grades better than his. It had depressed him at the start, but he had learned to accept it, as he had learned to accept many more situations in life. The thing to know was that a JC was not important. It was a mistake to have ever thought so. The price one paid for going to a missionary school with a motto and believing all that they told one. Education, Paul thought sardonically, it awes us as did the bicycle, the motorcar and the aeroplane. It is a Western thing and we throw away brother and sister for it but when it fails we are lost.

So he had not worried about his certificate getting lost. He had been thankful. It meant that he would not be tempted to pull it out next time they wanted somebody to work on the road and thus lose the job. He must forget that he was a JC. It used to embarrass him in the first days. He would approach those stuck-up gatekeepers who would ask him, 'What kind of job are you looking for?'

'A clerical job.'

'Oh, you educated boys! Everyone out of his mother's belly talks of being a clerk! Do you think Salisbury is run by an army of clerks? Why don't you be humble like me and go dig on the road?' They would gather round him and laugh.

It was much easier not to give any particulars about himself. He was a man looking for a job. While he had had shoes and decent trousers he had had confidence, but this had disappeared with the first nail in his now sole-less footwear and the first patch on the seat of his trousers. Decent clothes and the JC had put the burden of taking himself seriously on him.

Now, he was just anybody going for an interview.

They sat for the interview in a big tobacco shed rigged up for the moment as a classroom. There were fourteen of them. By their gloomy look of crushed bitter importance, he knew they were all JCs.

He came out first and got the job. The European who interviewed them said to him, 'You're going to start work on Monday. Be here at the office at seven sharp. I shall give you a letter to take to Mr Thomson.'

Paul guessed that Mr Thomson was the boss he was going to work for. The interview had been on a Friday. That Monday morning Paul came to collect the letter at the office.

'You'll find Mr Thomson in Number Four Shed.'

Paul took the letter to Mr Thomson — who immediately struck him as formidable. Paul could not think of anything to call him except a Rhodesian farmer. Mr Thomson was supervising a gang of workmen who were carrying tobacco bales to a truck waiting outside the shed.

'Excuse me . . .' Paul said, extending the right hand

with the letter.

'Yes? What do you want?' Mr Thomson turned towards Paul, annoyed. Paul saw the coarse open-air brick red face, the intimidating mossy-concrete-wall chest, and the hard, dusty-blue eyes under the wide-brimmed farmer hat with the lion-skin band round it.

'I was asked to give you this letter, sir,' Paul said, instinctively retreating.

Mr Thomson ignored the letter. 'Are you the bloke that's going to work with me?'

Paul did not quite catch the words and he brought his head forward and said, 'I beg your pardon, sir?'

Mr Thomson exploded. 'God! And a deaf one too! I said are you the bugger who is going to work for me?'

'I have been told to give you this letter, sir.'

'I'm not talking about your bloody letter. I can't read. All I want to know is whether you have come to work for me or not. A simple question. Can't you answer that?'

'I think I am the one, sir.'

'Haven't you been told?'

'I have been told, sir.'

'Then what the hell do you have to think for?'

'I thought. . .'

'Listen, chum.' A podgy index drummed Paul's chest. 'I don't want any bloody thinkers here. I want somebody to listen and obey orders and do what he's told. Don't tell me you think. I do all the thinking for all of you bunheads here and you listen and do, see? My, I think, I think. You think my ass.'

Mr Thomson turned away from him and walked towards a desk in a far corner of the shed. Paul remained standing where he was.

At his desk Mr Thomson bellowed across the shed,

41

'You ain't gonna stand there for all eternity, are you?'

Paul started quickly for the desk. He still held the letter in his hand. Mr Thomson pulled out a piece of paper and a pencil.

'Name?'

'Paul Masaga.'

'Worked in a tobacco-grading shed before?'

'No, sir.'

'Whaaat?'

'I haven't worked in. . .'

'Then what the devil have you come here for?' Mr Thomson banged the desk with his fist.

'I passed the interview, sir.'

'So, what's that to me? I don't give people interviews here. I give them work, work, work!'

'I have a JC, sir, and. . .'

'Listen, Mr Jay See. I said I want someone who knows tobacco-grading work. I should have said I wanted a JC if I had wanted that. Some people don't seem to listen. When did you leave school?'

'Two years ago.'

'What have you been doing since then?'

'I have been looking for a job.'

'Then if that's what you know why the hell don't you go on looking for a job? Come on, Jay See. Get out.'

'But . . . but. . .'

'Want me to throw you out?'

Paul turned and made for the door. He could hear Mr Thomson snorting behind him. At the door of the shed the workmen were in a group looking at him. He did not stop to answer their whispered questions.

He walked to the office. The European in the office looked up when Paul knocked at the door.

'Yes? Oh, it's you Paul. What is it now?'

'Mr Thomson said I am not experienced.'

'Balls! What's all this? He complains to me he wants people. I send him fifteen in a bloody week and he says they're not intelligent. Now I send him someone who is intelligent and he says he has no experience. Hell's teeth!'

The man lifted a phone and rang Mr Thomson.

'Mr Thomson? . . . Yes. Now, what's wrong with Paul? . . . Oh, but you didn't tell me. . . Yes. Aha. . . That's it, is it? Well, I'll be. . .' He dropped the receiver on its cradle.

He looked at Paul and said, 'Well, Paul, I'm sorry for all this. I tried my best but . . . well, I just don't know what's wrong with him. You know, we have never had people like you working for us before and I was beginning to think that now we might see something done at last. But it seems I should have . . . well, I really am sorry, Paul. For your trouble. . .'

The man was handing him a ten-shilling note. Paul accepted the money and thanked the man and went out. He could not think clearly. He was so used to Mr Thomson's type of settler that this other one came as a surprise to him and he did not know what to think.

He looked at the note. A crisp new note. The first he had owned in two years. He felt sad and generous. People cannot help being what they are, he said to himself. With tears of goodwill he forgave everybody for the misery in the world.

8

Coming of the Dry Season

ONE WEDNESDAY MOAB Gwati received a letter from Rusape. His mother was seriously ill. He decided to wait till he got his pay on Friday: Saturday he would go home.

He had his pay on Friday afternoon, and, as always happened with his money when he had it, it seemed to fly in all directions.

That Friday night he got hopelessly drunk with a girl he had picked up in Mutanga's earlier in the evening. Her name was Chipo but he did not know it till Sunday. They slept together in his room till eight o'clock Saturday morning.

He was still drunk and, after a cold shower he took together with Chipo, he ordered two quarts of Castle lager to take with their breakfast of fried liver and eggs.

After breakfast, with five other friends they drank till they dropped unconscious and their friends dumped them on the bed.

Early Sunday morning they had a beer and breakfast. They stayed in bed all morning. Moab felt his head beginning to ache. He had no more money and he did not want Chipo to know it.

At two o'clock he accompanied her to the bus station. He gave her a shilling for bus fare and a two-shilling piece for the fine weekend and patted her back in farewell. She said she had never been so happy in all her life. She stood in the queue to get on to the bus to Mufakose. Moab left before the ticket checker punched her ticket. As he was going away, the bus Chipo had taken passed him. He heard her yell and saw her wave to him. But he did not wave back. The black mood was on him.

When he felt this way Moab would walk for miles completely blind. It started always at the same emotional point, when, after a good time and he had no more money, he saw a gnarled old woman, thin as a starved cow, with a weak, saliva-flecked mouth and trembling limbs; very small dark eyes in carven sockets — a monkey face — and on her spare body threadbare rags wound as on a scarecrow stick. He would hear over and over the small mousy voice that was full of tears and self-pity, the voice that was a protest: 'Zindoga mwana'ngu, remember where you come from.' A warning, a remonstrance, a curse and an epitaph. With it, he could never have a good time in peace. Guilt, frustration and fury ate at his nerves.

When he spent four years without employment she had almost died from despair. She had cooked beer to the ancestors and then he told her he was working. And her health had improved. He knew that she had stood on her thin little legs and danced the *mbavarira*, which is both a praise to the ancestors and a prayer for the dead. He knew she had burned good luck roots for him.

It seemed he could never do enough for her. He had sent her money and clothes and a hundred-pound bag of mealie meal with his first pay. After this he had promised himself he would send her some more money — which he had done — yet there seemed no end to the things she needed. Her voice asked for far more than he could give. She had said once, when he had let her come to the city, 'Couldn't you find work somewhere near me? You know it won't be long and as you are my first born you must know all that you must do for me — for your own good — before I am gone. When I am gone you won't

45

ever set anything right by yourself.' There were many things wrong with the family, she had told him. And she had been glad that he was working now because he would be able to set them right and release her from bondage.

It had so depressed him that, wishing her gone, he had told her that one day he would take a leave and she would say all she wanted done and he would do it. He had told her to console herself and remember that she would be always in his thoughts. She had cried, whether for joy or sorrow, he had not known. But her tears had stayed with him and a guilt — about what he could not say — had dogged him like his shadow.

He smelled a sudden familiar smell. Dry, harvest-time smoke of burning maize-leaves. A shiver. Across the vlei the sun danced on the late red rapoko heads which nodded in the slight wind. In a pond of rust-coloured water rice was turning yellow and grass rotting in the pond stank. There had been unusually heavy rains this year. It was still raining, even now, in April. Another shiver. Why it should remind him of his mother, now very ill — at death's door as the letter had said — he did not know. He walked along the vlei, at the edge of Highfield Village. When he thought he should turn back, he entered Highfield from the west, having left it from the east.

He walked round and round Highfield. Night caught him still on the streets. Soon people left for bed and the dogs began their restless barking that would end with the coming of day.

In the northern sky he saw the bright arc of light that was the city. It reminded him of a veld fire at home. Only there was not the familiar smell of burning grass. If there had been, he knew he would have cried.

He watched the dogs trotting, mating, overturning bins

in search of left-overs, and relieving themselves on the streets. When he felt tired he went home.

The severe yellow light of his room, mixed with the strong smell of onions in dripping and rotting sofa sackcloth brought before him a prison cell and his mother. She was there now, imprisoned by life, trapped by her conscience, holding on tight till he was there to leave whatever it was she wanted to leave him. Her little cell, probably.

But she would have to let go without him. He had no money now. It was all finished. He switched off the light and lay on the bed unable to sleep till the milkman's bell. Lying in bed he heard rain falling. Thinking of his mother and a childhood belief he thought:

Soft earth
Wide spade
Are good friends.

He was listless the whole of the next day, a sunny Monday. His boss told him to take aspirin and go to bed, but he said he was all right. The boss, an understanding jovial man, had advised him not to take these weekends so severely.

Afraid of his yellow room, he slept at a friend's that night. On Tuesday, while walking to work, a bushy-tailed squirrel crossed and then recrossed his path. His heart sank. He asked for a sick leave that day and went home.

He found a telegram waiting for him next door where the postman had left it with his neighbours.

His mother had died on Saturday night.

Moab walked dazedly into his room. He sat in a chair and looked into a mean backyard of motorcar scraps and hen manure. He was thinking of nothing.

'Hello.'

It came weak and faraway as if it were his own

mother's voice greeting him from the grave. He turned towards the bed.

Chipo lay naked under a pink sheet. She smiled at him. For a long time he looked at her, dumb.

'I came yesterday evening. Your door was unlocked. I waited for you all night. Where have you been?' She sounded exactly like his mother. He hated her.

'Why have you come here? What do you want with me?'

Chipo looked confused, as if she had found herself, by mistake, in the Gents.

'But . . . but . . . you slept with me.'

'So what's that? Haven't you slept with many others? Why do you come to me?'

'But you are different. Moab, I wish you would marry me. I ask for nothing else.'

She looked at him sadly and her mouth twisted as if she had a pain somewhere. 'I have been alone too long.'

Suddenly he felt helpless, trapped. He said weakly, 'I did not ask you to come back.'

'I know. I just came back. You were so kind to me.'

He wondered what he had done for her. She was talking like his mother, suffering and saying things he did not understand. Why must they receive something else from what he intended to give — and then come back later to ask him for more of what he did not know how to give? He despised her. She had come back only to complicate his world.

'I don't have any more money,' he said harshly. 'That's what you want, isn't it? I don't have even a penny.'

'I know that, Moab. I didn't come for your money. I have too much of that.'

'Then why did you come back? Your type always comes back for money!' He glared at her.

48

She looked at him and did not answer. Her mouth twisted again, and there was a whiff of dry season air in the room. Moab's eyes filled.

'Go back where you come from! I didn't call you here!'

He stood up and yanked the sheet off her. She gasped but did not scream. She covered her private parts and hastily put on her dress. Moab noticed that her body was pitifully thin and starved.

He slumped back into his chair.

When she had finished putting on her clothes she took her handbag from a peg above the bed. From it she took a purse. Tilting the purse towards the light, so that Moab saw the thick wad of pound notes in it, Chipo extracted a shilling and a two-shilling piece and slapped them on the table beside Moab's right elbow. Then quietly she went out of the room.

Alone, Moab stared at the three shillings on the table. The ragged figure of his mother moved into focus. He felt damned.

His hand reached down for the money. He looked at it, wondering whether he should throw it out of the window on to the scrap heap. His head tightened and untightened with indecision: unclean money. But he had not even a penny in his pocket.

And his cheeks burning with shame, he furtively put the money into his pocket. He stood up and flung himself on the bed. He cried for something that was not the death of his mother.

9

S.O.S. from the Past

I MET HIM by accident at the bus stop as I was waiting for the bus into the city where I worked. I tried to avoid him and hoped that he would get on the bus before he saw me so that I could safely take the next one. But he saw me immediately and he must have noticed my eyes avoiding his.

'You haven't forgotten me, Mari?'

'No, Kasamba. How are you?'

'Fine. I thought you had forgotten.'

'I just hadn't noticed you.'

'Oh. I thought you were ignoring me. Ashamed of me. You know, many old friends from home do that when they are in the city these days.'

I said something and laughed.

'You are living here?'

'Yes.'

'With whom?'

'I am lodging at a friend's place.'

'Are you registered?'

'Yes.'

'So you are safe. It's hard living in the city these days — without a permanent place of your own.'

'The man I am staying with is all right.'

'Does he allow his lodgers to bring visitors into the house?'

'There are some lodgers who are staying with their relatives.'

'And he just lets them stay?'

'I haven't heard him say anything about them.'

'He is a good man.'

'He understands.'

'You see, I am staying with my brother-in-law. He built a room for me but the room is so small I can't get all my things into it. At present my wardrobe is in Harare with a friend, my radiogram is in Mufakose with another friend and all my clothes are with a third friend in Highfield. There is not enough space in my room. My bed fills up the whole place and I do my cooking on the verandah.'

'My room is quite big.'

'Look. Are there any more rooms still unoccupied in that house?'

'No.'

'That's a pity.'

The bus came and we got in. I hoped he would take another seat but he sat next to me.

'Do you write to Marara now?' Marara was Kasamba's brother and a childhood friend of mine. It was he, Marara, who was my friend and not Kasamba.

'No.'

'Why? Are you no longer friends?'

'We are. But we just don't write each other any more.'

'I think you should. The best friends are those from home. Only people from home can help you in time of need.'

I felt myself resisting his speech. All my life I had heard nothing but this kind of talk. And ever since I had been trying to run away from the trapping words of people from home. They said one thing and did another and always to my discredit. Whenever I went home it was always to hear my parents preach the same gospel, and listen to them accusing me of throwing them and my friends away. They always knew what I did in the city because people who worked there brought them news which was always bad news because I rarely met them or talked to them and did my best to avoid them. So they assumed that I was hiding something I wouldn't like my parents to hear of. So they went home, told my parents lies about me, and my parents, with tears for their prodigal son, and gratitude for these honest sons of other parents, fed them with beer and asked them more about me and gave them numerous messages which I always received a month or two old and over-exaggerated. I was tired of these stories of fights and scandals, hunger and misery from home. I wanted some quiet to do my own thinking and set things straight in my own mind before I threw in my lot with them and sold my soul to their gossip. You gave them beer to drink and they ended up by telling you everything about everybody at home. They made merciless judgements on people who were absent and innocent and when they went home you knew it was you who was judged, condemned and executed or exiled, all at a beer party. I couldn't be one of them and remain sane.

Now as Kasamba spoke I felt myself violently resisting all offers he made me. I had had too many offers and they had turned my nights into torture chambers and my days into concentration camps.

I half listened to him talking of home and how he had tried to forget his friends and parents and how all this had turned against him and now he was going to get married and build a home near his parents and let his wife look after the house while he worked here in the city. There was no life here in the city, he said.

When the bus got into the city I quickly climbed down and tried to shake him off. I was beginning to feel hunted — as I always felt when sometimes I doubted my own sanity and questioned my own behaviour towards friends, parents and relatives. The ghost of my guilt stalked the night of my soul and his voice had multiplied into a clamour: 'Save us, save us.' I wanted desperately to be rid of him.

But he stuck to me. He accompanied me to my place of work and talked ceaselessly for a half-hour as I waited for the shop to open at eight.

I had to tear myself away from him at five past eight after he had asked me whether I could fix him a place in the shop.

'No vacancy at the moment,' I said.

'If you want a dollar for your pains I can always square you up afterwards — if not here, at home. I can sell a chicken. . .'

'Never mind the money. I shall do my best.'

'Goodbye then. By the way, when do you go for your lunch?'

'One o'clock.'

'I shall call around then. I work quite near here.'

'All right. Now I must go to work.'

'Yes. Keep your work. Don't fight your superiors, you don't know all the answers.'

'Thank you.'

'See you at one.'

He was still standing outside the shop ten minutes later, looking up and down the street, and he was back at half-twelve, waiting for me to come out at one. His eyes were red and his lips were dry and he constantly ran his tongue over them. I knew he was not working but was ashamed to tell me.

I took him to a lunch bar and bought him a coke and a plate of sadza. I ate a hamburger and drank a lemonade.

Over lunch he told me he was really out of employment and was desperately in need of money to finish paying up for his wife. He had sold all his property to pay his accounts and now his wife had gone back to her parents, and they wouldn't let her come back until he had finished lobola.

'It's true that I'm living with my brother-in-law — but you know how it is with these brothers-in-law. He tells his friends that I'm lazy. I don't want to bend my back to honest work — all sorts of things he says when I am away and when I am there he pretends he likes me and tells me I can stay with him as long as I want. But I am tired now, Mari.'

We ate in silence then he said, 'How about me staying with you until I'm settled? I only want a place to sleep in. I know I will be all right in a week or two. You are from home and you are my friend, you understand. I shall help you too one day, you know.'

I felt my soul sink and my mind stretch with agony. Despite all my resolutions and rebelliousness I was still a coward.

'All right,' I said.

'Thank you. I shall help you one day. . .'

'Forget about that.'

I said goodbye to him after lunch and left him sitting in the bar. He looked very tired and I knew he would sit in there until five o'clock when I would come out of the shop and take him home.

10

The Accident

A MAN CARRYING a packet of tomatoes was knocked down by a car as he was crossing Cripps Road. He travelled in the air for twenty feet before he dropped to the side of the road. No one actually saw him hit.

He fell on his left side and face and did not move. His thigh was broken and twisted under him so that the foot faced backwards. His left arm lay twisted under him and the right was flung out backwards, palm up, as if he was asking for something. His grey socks had holes in them through which his yellow toes showed. One shoe lay on its side near his head. A piece of soiled cardboard which had been used to plug a hole in the sole of the shoe hung out like a tired dog's tongue. Further down the road the other shoe sat on the road as if it wanted to go somewhere.

His khaki trousers had been ripped at the back and nobody minded his dirty underwear which was soaking with blood. Blood came out of his mouth in a thick trickle and made a dark puddle on the sand. The distended nostrils were choked with more blood. By the slow up and down movement of his humped body people knew he was still alive but was having difficulty in breathing.

The European from the car came striding up the road. People turned to look at him. They watched him bend over the victim, then without touching him, he straightened his back and wiped his face. People could not read his face. It was difficult to read European faces. But they all noticed that the man wiped his face although there was no sweat on it. They noticed that he was short, thickset, with a bullneck that supported a big head. They noticed that he had hair round the sides of his head and in front near the forehead but none on the top of his head. And the strands of hair in front were brushed back, to cover the bald crown maybe, but later, as the people watched, the straggly strands of hair fell over his face, leaving the top as bare and red as an overripe tomato. Later, too, they noticed that something in his temple vibrated, minutely, like the wing of a mosquito alighted on a glass pane.

But in his face they could not read anything. They felt he was indifferent. Then they began to talk, in tones of suppressed sorrow and anger, and this grew in volume and intensity as more people came and stood on both sides of the road.

Most people took one look at the victim, covered their faces with their hands and did not look again but waited to hear the story. Without being told they knew that the European had done it. He was alone there and it was logical that it should be him.

The European stood a few feet from the victim, surrounded by the crowd whose language he did not know but whose feeling he understood. He did not look at them. Once, he lifted his head, and above the people's heads, looked up Cripps Road in the direction of the town. The red stop glare a hundred yards up the road returned his stare. Slowly he lowered his head to its original position. Two minutes later, almost imperceptibly, his head turned again to look down the road. He saw more and more Africans coming. No Europeans. Three minutes later he brushed his brow with his fingers as if he had a headache. His left arm hung straight down his side, fingers clenched.

Around him, the crowd thickened and the talk that he did not understand hissed on like steam under pressure.

Cars passed by, changing down to dead slow as they approached the crowd, and picking up brutal speed past the people. And always in those cars that passed the people would catch sight of the stiff-necked, ahead-looking head of some indifferent or frightened European. There was only one old European woman who put her hands to her face and the man who was driving with her put his arm around her shoulders.

African drivers stopped their cars a little way past the crowd and came back to look and ask questions and stare and condemn. Those of them who did not see the European at first would ask, 'Who did it?'

'That Boer.'

'Which is his car?'

'That one down the road, with the broken windscreen.'

'He did it on purpose. I saw it all. This man', pointing to the victim, 'stopped to let the car pass but the bloody baboon went out of his way to kill him.' The speaker was a young man in a straw hat who had come much later after the man had been hit.

An old woman said, 'That's why I said to my son, "You aren't going anywhere. You stay here in the reserve with me. Who is there to tell me when this happens?" No, my son stays at home.'

The youth in the straw hat said, 'The man was not in his way at all. He was just carrying his tomatoes home. His wife is probably wondering why he has delayed so.'

'Oh, they don't care.'

'The bloody beasts.'

There was a silence. A wind blew down the road. A piece of dirty newspaper glided with the faintest rustle along the tarmac. It was caught by the man's bleeding

57

head. Another gust came again. The paper freed itself, left the man, and glided further down the road. Past the crowd the paper rose into the air and sailed away over the Shawasha Men's Hostels to the west.

The man who said he had seen it all went on talking as if he was appealing to the people to do something. 'He was just standing beside the road not talking to anybody and this maniac comes along and knocks him down.'

The crowd was increasing. The European looked round and then walked down the road with short, nervous steps, his hands hanging by his sides. The people's eyes were on him all the way to his car.

'Is that him?'

'Yes. That's the murderer. I was standing talking to the man when this — Boer knocked him down. I am going to say all I saw exactly as I saw it to the police.'

'They won't listen to you.'

'But I shall have said my share. I shall have shown them that they can't get away with everything here.'

'They have got away with much worse before.'

'But this time they won't.'

'They will. Until you rule them.'

'He wants to go away?' somebody asked, looking at the European who was now standing beside his car. They saw him look up and down the road, then bend into his car and search for something on the front seat. Nobody said anything. They just watched him with a silence that clearly said: You can't go away. The man straightened his back and blew his nose. Again he looked up and down the road. Then reluctantly he was heavy-stepping back to the dying man, adjusting sunglasses on his face. It was then that the people saw the mosquito-wing vibration in his temple.

There was a shrill shriek up the road. Heads turned.

'The police,' somebody whispered.

There was a slight backward-falling in the crowd, as the police landrover skidded to a dusty stop beside the dying man. Two policemen, a European and his African assistant, jumped out.

While the African constable pushed the crowd back on both sides of the road the European policeman studied the victim and wrote in a notebook. The other European moved nearer the policeman and looked on. Both of them were looking at the victim in silence. Then they were speaking in very low, almost friendly tones, the people thought.

'Blood is thicker than water,' somebody in the crowd said.

'Oh, they dare not let him go. I saw it all.' As if to confirm his statement the young man in the straw hat moved to the front line of the crowd, nearest the two Europeans and the victim.

'He did it on purpose!' the young man shouted for the benefit of the Europeans.

'Shut up, you!' The African constable glared at the youth. There was a sudden dangerous rumble in the crowd and somebody said, 'You don't drink with them. Remember that!'

The two Europeans did not turn their heads. The policeman went on taking notes while the other stared at the dying man and murmured something. The African constable moved round keeping the crowd well back from the road and the victim. He was not saying anything since somebody had told him to remember that he did not drink with the Europeans.

There was another shriek and, emergency light on the roof blipping, the ambulance stopped on the other side of the victim so that he was now between the two cars,

The white-coated driver jumped out, opened the back of the van and pulled out a stretcher. More people than were really necessary from the crowd stepped forward to help lift the man on to the stretcher and into the ambulance.

The two Europeans looked on, saying nothing. After the ambulance had driven off, they walked side by side down the road to the killer car. Then with the crowd's eyes on them, the Europeans walked back again to the police car.

The policeman spoke. 'Is there anyone who saw this man knocked down?'

The youth in the straw hat stepped forward, and without taking off his hat, said, 'I saw everything. I saw the man knocked down.'

'You sure?' the policeman asked, narrowing his eyes with a sideways glance at the African constable, who interpreted the question into vernacular.

'Sure. I saw everything.' The youth's face showed no expression.

'All right. Stand there. Anybody else?' Again the African constable translated and added that nobody should step forward who had not seen the man actually hit. There were derisive rumbles from the crowd and two other young men defiantly stepped forward. It looked as if more were prepared to hand themselves over but the constable held up his hand and said, 'Enough.'

'You saw the man knocked down?'

'Yes, Nkosi.'

'Are you sure?'

'Yes, Baas.'

'Good. You will give your names to constable Tayengwa and you will come with us for a statement at the police station.'

'Yes, sir.'

After the witnesses' names had been taken the police car drove off, followed by the killer car.

When they had gone there was a silence in the crowd, a disappointed silence.

'He's going to be released.'

'But those three men have courage. If only we had ten more like them — men who can stand up and tell them that they are wrong.'

'It will be a long, long time before we have ten like that.'

'We have them, only. . .' And arguing sad politics the crowd dispersed, all going in the same direction, south-west, into the location. They all felt the same thing: once again, nothing has happened.

Other books by Charles Mungoshi
In the ZPH Writers series:

Waiting for the Rain

'Things are happening here and there and whether you can see them or not you can't certainly say the Old Man doesn't see them.

The air trembles with roaring thunder and the earth grumbles with earthquakes and shrieking lightning splits the darkness into quivering shreds of light and he is a lonely whirling little dot who has to hold his own to stay alive. Way, way ahead of him is a pinpoint flash which keeps on going farther and farther, but it's all right — the distance is always the same despite sensations of now being very far away and cold and lonely. And there is this nameless thing, a feeling, akin to hunger, but again you know that this passes too, just as so many things have passed without you doing anything about them. Or — does it pass? He is not sure. Sometimes he is certain that it doesn't pass. He wants it so much to pass that he thinks it's gone when it really is still there. Still there, under everything else — so many things happening at the same time — enough to make one's head snap and spin. It is under there, together with the feeling of being very near to, and involved in, the pulsing and flashing brilliant centre. This is the Old Man's drum.'

www.ingramcontent.com/pod-product-compliance
Lightning Source LLC
Chambersburg PA
CBHW051147020726
47501CB00005B/1706